A Charlie Brown
Valentine

LITTLE SIMON

An imprint of Simon & Schuster Children's Publishing Division
1230 Avenue of the Americas, New York, New York 10020
Copyright © 2002 by United Feature Syndicate, Inc. All rights reserved.
All rights reserved, including the right of reproduction in whole or in part in any form.
LITTLE SIMON and colophon are registered trademarks of Simon & Schuster.
Manufactured in the United States of America
ISBN 0-689-87742-0

Adapted from the works of Charles M. Schulz

A Charlie Brown
Valentine™

By Charles M. Schulz
Adapted by Justine and Ron Fontes
Illustrated by Paige Braddock
Based on the television special produced by
Lee Mendelson and Bill Melendez

LITTLE SIMON

New York   London   Toronto   Sydney   Singapore

Valentine's Day was on its way. The whole Peanuts gang was dizzy with visions of lacy love notes, secret admirers, and chocolates.

Even Marcie had valentines on her mind. She told her friend Peppermint Patty that she was planning to send one to Charlie Brown.

"You can't do that! He'll think you like him," Peppermint Patty warned.

"I do . . . I'm very fond of Charles," Marcie replied.

Suddenly Peppermint Patty realized she also liked Charlie Brown!

But who did Charlie Brown like? Marcie knocked on his door and said, "I may or may not be sending you a valentine, Charles, so I need to know something. Do you like me?"

Charlie Brown was too surprised to answer. "Do I what?"

Marcie fumed. "I walk all the way over here to ask you a question and all you can say is, 'Do I what?' Forget it, Charles."

Now Charlie Brown was even more confused. "Forget what?"

Charlie Brown did get a love letter after all. With a secret smile on her face, Peppermint Patty watched him read it.

"'I know you like me, and in my own way I like you, too, but . . .'" Charlie Brown's heart beat faster as he read. Could the girl of his dreams finally have noticed him? He turned to Peppermint Patty and said, "I think it's from the Little Red-Haired Girl. She knows I like her and—"

Peppermint Patty shouted, "That's not from the Little Red-Haired Girl, Chuck! That letter is from ME! You like ME, Chuck!"

Again, Charlie Brown was surprised. "I do?"

But Charlie Brown knew his heart belonged to the Little Red-Haired Girl. And this year he was determined to give her a valentine! Charlie Brown told his sister, Sally, his plan and showed her the valentine.

Sally said, "She'll probably laugh in your face."

Charlie Brown sighed. "At least I'd be near her!"

Charlie Brown showed the valentine to Snoopy.

"I want to go to the Little Red-Haired Girl's house and give this valentine to her," he said. "But I'd be too nervous without practice. I'll go outside and ring the doorbell, and you pretend you're the Little Red-Haired Girl, okay?"

Charlie Brown clutched the valentine, walked up to the door, rang the bell, and . . .

RING!

. . . there stood Snoopy in a bright red wig!

Since Snoopy was no help, Charlie Brown decided to rehearse on his own. On the way to the Little Red-Haired Girl's house, he practiced what he would say: "Here, Little Red-Haired Girl, I made this valentine especially for you. . . . Here, this valentine is for you, sweet Little Red-Haired Girl. . . ." He tried out different smiles and even a wink.

He wondered if she really would laugh in his face like Sally said, or if she'd throw the valentine back at him, or . . . Charlie Brown couldn't stand it anymore. He mailed his valentine to the Little Red-Haired Girl—and he didn't even sign it!

Next Charlie Brown decided to buy the Little Red-Haired Girl some candy for Valentine's Day. He told the store clerk, "I'd like to buy a box of candy for a girl who doesn't know I exist."

When the clerk asked him what kind of candy, Charlie Brown explained, "Nothing too expensive, ma'am. I'll never have the nerve to give it to her anyway."

But he had to try! Charlie Brown walked all the way to the Little Red-Haired Girl's house with the candy. He stopped at the tree near her door and thought, Maybe I can hide behind this tree.

When she comes by, I'll hold out the box and she'll take it out of my hand. He sighed. "Love makes you do strange things."

Charlie Brown couldn't sleep! He kept thinking about the Little Red-Haired Girl. Tomorrow I'll come right out and tell her I love her, he decided. Then I'll give her a big hug and . . .

Who was he kidding? He was Charlie Brown! He was as likely to confess his love to the Little Red-Haired Girl as he was to bungee jump off the moon.

The next day at recess Charlie Brown saw the Little Red-Haired Girl! "Maybe I should invite her to the Valentine's Dance," he said to his friend Linus. Charlie Brown's stomach flip-flopped. "Do me a favor. Go over and try to find out if she likes me. I'll hide behind this trash can and listen."

Charlie Brown listened as Linus described him to the Little Red-Haired Girl. "He sits across the room from you. No, by the window . . . Near the pencil sharpener . . . No, in the last row. Sort of a round face . . . Doesn't ring a bell, huh? No, 'Brown,' like in 'town.'"

Charlie Brown sank to the ground with a broken heart. The Little Red-Haired Girl didn't even know who he was!

Lucy thought Charlie Brown should simply introduce himself. But Charlie Brown explained, "I can't talk to the Little Red-Haired Girl. She has a pretty face, and pretty faces make me nervous."

Lucy roared, "How come *my* face doesn't make you nervous, huh?! I have a pretty face! How come you can talk to me?!"

Charlie Brown hurried home before Lucy could get any madder. He decided to write a letter to the Little Red-Haired Girl. That would be easier than talking to her. He asked Sally if she would deliver the love note for him.

Sally fretted. "If I get captured, do I have to swallow it?"

Finally Sally agreed to take the note to the Little Red-Haired Girl. Charlie Brown waited nervously behind a tree.

"Should I wait for an answer?" Sally yelled back to her brother.

Charlie Brown fainted from embarrassment.

RING!

Charlie Brown sat up, still worrying. What would the Little Red-Haired Girl think of his note? Would she laugh? Would she go to the dance with him? Could she possibly love him too?

Sally handed Charlie Brown back his note. "She said she couldn't read your smudgy writing." On the way home Sally added, "And when I told her you're in the same class, she said she didn't remember you."

Charlie Brown sighed. "I can't stand it!"

"Why don't you invite her to the Valentine's Dance right now?" Linus asked at lunch the next day.

Charlie Brown explained. "I can't talk to the Little Red-Haired Girl. She's something and I'm nothing. If I were something and she were nothing, I could talk to her. Or if she were something and I were something. Or if she were nothing and I were nothing—"

Linus interrupted. "You know, Charlie Brown, for a nothing, you're really something."

Back in the classroom Charlie Brown tried winking at the Little Red-Haired Girl. She didn't seem to notice. So he winked harder. Charlie Brown winked so hard that the teacher sent him to the eye doctor!

"Why don't you get her phone number and call her to invite her to the dance?" Linus suggested.

Charlie Brown's hands were shaking so hard, he dialed the wrong number. He called Marcie by mistake!

Marcie recognized Charlie Brown's voice right away. "I'll bet you dialed my number by mistake, didn't you, Charles? I'll bet you meant to call Peppermint Patty. She happens to be right here. I'll put her on."

"No! Wait! I—," Charlie Brown yelled. But it was too late.

"Hi, Chuck!" Peppermint Patty said. "Finally got up the nerve to call me, eh? I bet you called to invite me to the Valentine's Dance. Well, I accept."

Charlie Brown didn't know what to do. He had tried to call the Little Red-Haired Girl, but somehow wound up having a date with Peppermint Patty. He had the Charlie Browniest luck in the world!

On Valentine's Day, Charlie Brown put on his dancing clothes and went to feed Snoopy. He found his dog all dressed-up for the dance too.

"How will you get into the dance?" Charlie Brown asked. "Dogs aren't invited."

Snoopy winked and danced. How could anyone so dashing *not* get into the dance?

Still, the boy at the door tried to turn Snoopy away. "This is a dance! The dog can't come in!" "This little kid thought it was a costume ball, so he wore a dog suit," Charlie Brown explained. It worked! Charlie Brown and Snoopy walked toward the dance floor. Charlie Brown hoped he would have a chance to dance with the Little Red-Haired Girl. Sure enough, she was there!

"She's just waiting for you to ask her to dance," Linus said.

Charlie Brown's knees shook. His heart pounded with every step. "I'm going to ask her to dance. . . . I'm getting closer. . . . I'm almost there. . . . I'm . . ."

Suddenly Marcie and Peppermint Patty grabbed him and pulled him onto the dance floor.

"We've been looking for you, Chuck!" said Peppermint Patty.

They danced the Hokey Pokey until the music finally stopped.

Linus rushed up to Charlie Brown. "It's the last dance!"
This was Charlie Brown's last chance. He looked over at the Little
Red-Haired Girl and saw . . .

. . . that she was already dancing
with Snoopy!

Charlie Brown sighed. "Good grief!"

The next day Charlie Brown looked at his mailbox sadly. Another Valentine's Day is over, he thought to himself. I'd give anything if that Little Red-Haired Girl had sent me a valentine.

Then a happy idea occurred to him: Maybe she did, but it was delayed in the mail. Maybe it's in the box right now—a real fancy one with lace and perfume! Charlie Brown opened the mailbox and . . .

. . . Snoopy popped out and gave him a big, doggy kiss!

Then the beagle bounced out of the mailbox and started dancing. Charlie Brown and Linus danced too!

There were no valentines from the Little Red-Haired Girl, but that was all right. When you're Charlie Brown, you don't really expect too much. It's enough to have good friends, a faithful (if crazy) dog, and a heart full of love and hope.

Linus shouted, "Happy Valentine's Day, Charlie Brown!"

And it was.